A BIG TRIP FOR
The Morrisons

By Penny Carter

Viking

VIKING
Published by the Penguin Group
Penguin Books USA Inc., 375 Hudson Street, New York, New York 10014, U.S.A.
Penguin Books Ltd, 27 Wrights Lane, London W8 5TZ, England
Penguin Books Australia Ltd, Ringwood, Victoria, Australia
Penguin Books Canada Ltd, 10 Alcorn Avenue, Toronto, Ontario, Canada M4V 3B2
Penguin Books (N.Z.) Ltd, 182-190 Wairau Road, Auckland 10, New Zealand

Penguin Books Ltd, Registered Offices: Harmondsworth, Middlesex, England

First published in 1997 by Viking, a division of Penguin Books USA Inc.

1 3 5 7 9 10 8 6 4 2

LIBRARY OF CONGRESS CATALOGING-IN-PUBLICATION DATA
Carter, Penny.
A big trip for the Morrisons / by Penny Carter.
p. cm.
Summary: The Morrisons visit China, France, Italy, and other
countries, always finding something they do not like.
ISBN 0-670-87022-6 (hardcover)
[1. Voyages and travels—Fiction. 2. Geography—Fiction.]
I. Title.
PZ7.C2477Bi 1997
[E]—dc21 96-52796 CIP AC

Manufactured in China
Set in Weidemann Medium

To Robin

The Morrisons were going on a trip.
They were very excited.
"I'm ready," said Albert.

Their friends helped them carry their bags,
then drove them to the airport.

"We will visit many places," Mrs. Morrison told them.
"It will be so much fun," added Mr. Morrison.

"We show our tickets here," Mrs. Morrison said.
Albert waved good-bye.

Mr. and Mrs. Morrison did not like the airplane.
"Our seats are too small," Mrs. Morrison said.
"Can't we go any faster?" asked Mr. Morrison.

First the Morrisons visited China.

"There are too many tourists," Mr. Morrison said.

Then they went to France.

"The food is strange," said Mrs. Morrison.

"In Italy the streets are full of water," they said.

They went on to India.

"The taxi is too slow," Mr. Morrison said.

"Russia is too cold."

"Egypt is too hot."

Off they went to Austria.

"I don't like this music," said Mrs. Morrison.

Then they visited Hawaii.

"I *really* don't like this music," Mr. Morrison said.

"Too much rain."

"Too much sun."

"We want to go home!" said Mr. and Mrs. Morrison.

At last they reached the airport.
Their friends were waiting for them.
"How was your trip?" they asked.

"We went to so many places," Mrs. Morrison told them.
"We tried so many new things," added Mr. Morrison.
"It really was a lot of fun," Mrs. Morrison said.
"Yes," Mr. Morrison said, "it was a great trip."

"Let's take *another* trip!" said Mrs. Morrison.
"Great idea!" Mr. Morrison said.
"I'll call the travel agent right away!"
"I'm ready," said Albert.